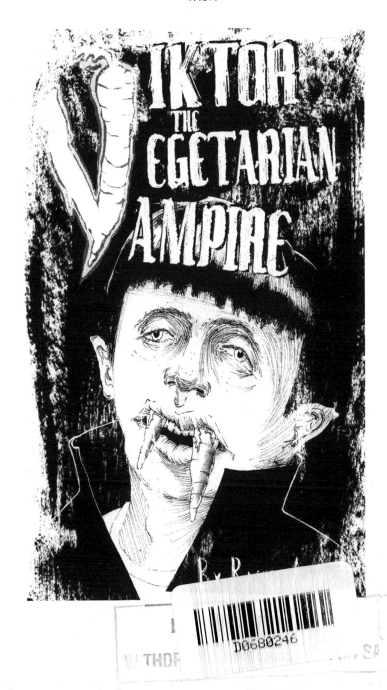

ISBN: 978-1-5142710-5-6

Front jacket cover design: Louis R.A. Labron-Johnson
Book design: Dean Fetzer, www.gunboss.com

My warmest thanks to Harry Bingham, Emily Diamand, Heather Dyer, Shaun McCarthy and Julia Wallis Martin for their help, support and encouragement and to Louis R.A. Labron-Johnson for his imaginative interpretation of my idea for the cover.

*In loving memory of*
*Anna Standon*

# CHAPTER 1

"**N**O FANGS!" cried Evilina Vicious. "No fangs! What do you mean '*No fangs*'? Viktor's nearly a hundred years old. They should be through by now."

"I'll show you," said Mr. Sharpe the dentist. He turned to the tiny figure that seemed lost in the huge chair.

Viktor had been trembling from the moment his mother brought him into the gloomy surgery that lay deep below St. Chad's churchyard. But, when he looked up at the dentist's massive shape looming over him and saw that the white pattern on his dark suit was made from real teeth, he began to shake.

Mr. Sharpe let down the back of the chair so suddenly that Viktor lay like an upturned beetle with his legs waving in the air. Above him he could see the roots of an old yew tree that had grown through the surgery ceiling. And the sight of the sharp-looking instruments dangling from them made him clench his teeth.

"Snarl please," said Mr. Sharpe.

1

Viktor curled his lips and opened his mouth slightly.

"Wider!" said Mr. Sharpe. "Now, don't move."

He placed a piece of snail shell behind Viktor's top teeth and, as he peered at his gums, the dentist's pink eyes turned to a glowing red.

"Look at this X-ray, Mrs. Vicious," he said, showing her the piece of shell. "It's not just that his fangs aren't showing yet – there are no signs of any coming through. It is very strange. Never known anything like it!"

"But where are they?" said Evilina. "As I told you, Viktor's nearly a hundred years old and soon it'll be time for his First Flight."

"If I were you," said Mr. Sharpe, "I'd have a word with the doctor. She may know what's holding things up and suggest some treatment. I've taken an impression of his upper jaw – his wisdom fangs on his lower jaw won't be through for another fifty years – and I could make him a bridge with some false fangs. Then he wouldn't look…well…so human-like."

"I'll let you know when I've spoken to Dr. Pearce," said Evilina.

Viktor was silent as they walked along the broad tunnel that ran right through Vampsville.

Human-like? he thought. I've seen human faces on their telly and they seem rounder with more colour than ours.

# Viktor the Vegetarian Vampire

There are no mirrors in the vampires' world because they have no reflections so Viktor wasn't exactly sure what he looked like.

Perhaps it's because I look different, he thought, the others don't want to play with me at break-time or have me in their group in class. I've always pretended I didn't mind but I can't go on pretending after that poem.

Someone had pushed the poem, scratched on a dry leaf, into his locker the day they broke up for half-term.

> *Viktor the vimp*
> *Is really a wimp*
> *Who's scared of blood and bangs.*
> *When offered a bite*
> *He always takes fright*
> *And runs away saying 'No fangs!'*

By the time he came to the end his eyes were so full of tears he could scarcely read. He'd crushed the leaf to dust but he couldn't destroy the words – they were burned into his brain.

He hadn't told Evilina about it because he wanted her to think he was doing well at school. But somehow she'd found out the truth and made an appointment with Mr. Sharpe. And now Mr. Sharpe had said he *was* different from the others.

Evilina was silent too which wasn't like her – she usually had plenty to say, her flame-red hair

3

bouncing with energy when she spoke. But, glancing sideways, Viktor noticed her hair lay lankly on her drooping shoulders and he knew that meant she was thinking. Suddenly she said,

"How would you feel about a bridge with fangs?"

"Sounds uncomfortable."

"Oh I don't know. I'm sure Mr. Sharpe would see it fitted properly. And it might help you."

"How?" said Viktor.

"Well, like Mr. Sharpe said, it would…it would…make you look more like…the other vimps at school.

"As it's half-term, why don't you invite some of them round?" she said as they turned down the narrow tunnel that led to their home.

"N-o thanks."

"Why not?"

"I…I…I've got too much homework."

"Better get started then," she said when they got in. "What do you have to do?"

"We've got to watch a horror film on human telly. Supposed to show us some of their stupid ideas about us vampires."

"Human beings *are* stupid. They think we lie in our tombs all day. They don't understand that the tombs are just doorways to our comfortable homes down here," said Evilina, stroking the moss-covered sofa and looking round at the dried wreaths she'd brought back from the graveyard to decorate their earth walls.

Viktor nodded. He remembered the locked door near Evilina's bedroom. She'd opened it once to show him that it led to a staircase.

"That goes up to our tomb but you won't need to use it till you're fully-blooded after your First Bite," she'd said.

Viktor switched on the television. The words 'Dracula Bites Again' appeared on the screen in large Gothic letters while, in the background, bats flew over a hilltop castle in the moonlight.

Viktor yawned. He knew the gardening programme 'Down to Earth' was coming up on another channel. He'd seen it the week before and they'd said that the next time they'd be harvesting fruit and vegetables with Flora Digweed on her allotment.

"This film is bo-oring," he said to his mother.

"Lucky to have television," said Evilina. "When we were at school we had to learn everything from books. Now we can tap into their underground cables things are a lot easier. You get a better idea of what to expect. And I must say I enjoy their hospital dramas – always lots of blood. I'm going upstairs to rest. I need to think over what Mr. Sharpe said."

As soon as she left the room, Viktor switched channels.

# CHAPTER 2

After some cheerful music the smiling face of a rosy-cheeked woman appeared.

"A warm welcome all our green-fingered viewers," said Flora.

"Green!" echoed Viktor. "Green! At school they said human skin can be black, brown, yellow or pink but they didn't saying anything about their fingers being green. Weird!"

He loved looking at the bright colours of the human world. Compared with them everything in Vampsville seemed like the old black and white films he'd seen on television. He sighed as he watched people working in the bright sunshine. He knew he could never see real sunshine – even daylight is dangerous for vampires – but he was safe looking at it on the screen.

"Today we've been joined by the winner of our 'Why I'd like an allotment' essay competition," said Flora turning to a young girl standing beside her. "Margaret, can you tell our viewers why?"

With her soft brown hair, round eyes and small

nose which twitched from time to time she reminded Viktor of a little mouse he'd once seen in a nature programme.

"It's…it's because I'm a vegetarian," said Margaret. "And fruit and veg. cost a lot in the shops."

"I think you'd find your own would taste better too. They'd be fresher as they wouldn't have travelled so far," said Flora. "Now, if anyone would like to phone in to ask Margaret a question, our number is at the bottom of the screen."

Without taking his eyes from the television, Viktor backed towards the door, opened it and picked up the phone on the hall table, just outside the room. He rang the number and gave his name to the operator.

"Our first caller," said Flora, "is Viktor. Where are you speaking from Viktor?"

Viktor didn't know what to say. Should he say 'Underground'? "Mmm. Grrunnd," he mumbled.

"The line's very poor," said Flora. "Did you say Gravesend?"

"…Ye-es," said Viktor. "Near there."

"Go ahead, Viktor. What do you want to ask Margaret?"

"What…what…what's a vegetarian?" said Viktor, thinking how strange it was to hear his own voice coming back at him from the television.

"Someone who doesn't eat meat or fish," said Margaret. "You see I don't like the idea of putting dead animals into my mouth."

"So is that why you eat a lot of fruit and veg.?" said Viktor. "What's your favourite fruit?"

"Raspberries," said Margaret.

"You're in luck," said Flora. "Ours are ripe."

There was a close-up of some juicy red berries which seemed to glow against their green leaves.

"Try some," said Flora.

Margaret reached out, picked one and popped it into her mouth, then another and another. When she turned back to face the camera there was a huge red stain round her mouth.

"We've another caller," said Flora.

"Bye, Viktor. I'd like to tell you more about being a vegetarian some time," said Margaret, giving him a little wave.

Viktor waved at the screen and went back into the room, closing the door behind him.

Wonder what eating feels like? he thought, remembering the time at school when they'd been shown a picture of an ice cream and he'd said, "Ooh! That looks good!"

And he'd been made to write a hundred times VAMPIRES NEVER EAT.

The raspberries on the screen looked delicious. He wished Evilina would give him a transfusion of red raspberries instead of his morning transfusion of blood that often made him sick.

"Why do I have to have transfusions?" he'd asked her.

"All vimps need them till they're old enough to collect blood for themselves," she'd replied.

Viktor scarcely listened to the other callers.

"I've talked to a human being," he said to himself. "None of the other vimps at school have done that. Wish I could tell them about it but they'd only laugh at me if they knew the sort of programmes I watch."

He went on looking at Margaret's big red mouth. She's nice, he thought, I'd like to be friends with her.

"Doesn't sound like a horror film!" shouted Evilina from the other side of the door.

Viktor switched channels quickly. To the sound of whining music a dark, cloaked figure flew out of a castle window with blood dripping from its jaws, saying, "Ha! Ha! Ha!"

"Oh, ha,ha,ha," muttered Viktor. "It's not funny. It's dead boring! I want to get back to Margaret and those raspberries."

He waited for a few minutes and then went to the door to listen, hoping Evilina would have gone. But he heard her speaking on the phone.

"I'd like an appointment with Dr. Pearce as soon as possible. I'm very worried about my vimp Viktor."

# CHAPTER 3

"**N**ow then, Viktor," said Dr. Pearce, staring at him through her dark-rimmed glasses, "what seems to be the problem?"

Viktor hung his head.

"Smfangs," he mumbled.

"It's his fangs!" said Evilina.

"Open wide and say 'Ah'," said Dr. Pearce, pushing a long thin bone down his throat.

"A-a-argh!" gasped Viktor as she leaned over him and peered into his mouth.

"Hm. Don't seem to be through yet," she said.

"That's the problem and it's not the only one…Viktor go and read one of those books," said Evilina, pointing to a pile at the far end of the room.

Good, thought Viktor. Don't like being poked and prodded. It's bad enough her pushing that bone down my throat but pressing her pointy nose and chin into my face is worse.

He picked up a copy of 'Impelling Impaling' and pretended to read. But though Evilina and Dr.

Pearce lowered their voices he could still hear most of what they said.

"I don't know where to begin," said Evilina. "I think the trouble started after his father Vlad… didn't…didn't…come home."

"Tell me about it," said Dr. Pearce.

"We-ell. We took it in turns to collect blood while the other looked after Viktor. One night Vlad went out as soon as it was dark. But when he didn't come back I went to the top of our stairs. Our tomb must have still been open because I could hear, very faintly, a cock crow…and…and…then I knew Vlad must have got caught by the first light of dawn."

Dr. Pearce's mind could read her patients' thoughts just as Mr. Sharpe's eyes could see through their gums so she knew what had really happened. But the words STAKE THROUGH THE HEART are so terrible that no polite vampire will say them aloud. She nodded. "Go on Evilina," she said, writing S.T.T.H. in her notes.

"Since then I've noticed Viktor's not…well, not like other vimps. He's often sick after his morning transfusion. And I know he's watching some very strange television programmes because I've listened at the door when he's supposed to be doing his homework."

She gulped and stopped for a moment while Dr. Pearce waited till she was ready to go on.

"When I spoke to the head teacher, Mr. Fear, I found that things were worse than I'd thought. He told me Viktor is frightened of screams, loud noises and sharp pointed objects. And he has weird ideas, saying he wants to 'EAT FOOD' and 'BE FRIENDS WITH HUMAN BEINGS'!

"I do hope he's not taking after my husband's sister, Bloodjilly. I never met her but Vlad told me she used to talk like that. And," said Evilina, dropping her voice to a whisper, "on her First Flight she...she ate something...and became a human being. I think Vlad visited her once but he'd never talk about it."

Dr. Pearce looked through her records. "Ah, yes" she said. "I remember her mother bringing her in. But Bloodjilly had no problems with her fangs or transfusions."

Evilina sighed and sat silent for a while. Then she took a deep breath and went on,

"Mr. Fear said he doesn't think Viktor will be ready to go on the First Flight with the others not just because of the strange things he says but also because his fangs haven't developed yet. And the only thing Mr. Sharpe could suggest was a bridge with false fangs."

She began to cry. Little pink tears rolled down her pale cheeks.

"Have you tried talking to him about it?" asked Dr. Pearce, passing her a box of cobwebs. Evilina took one and dried her eyes.

"Oh I couldn't. He doesn't know I've found out how bad things are at school."

She doesn't know *just* how bad things are at school, thought Viktor.

At first he'd enjoyed learning about the weird world of humans. He'd looked forward to exploring it and making friends with the people who lived there. But, when he realised they were only learning how to make friends with human beings in order to suck their blood, he was very upset.

He was surprised that none of the other vimps felt like he did. He'd stand near them in the playground and hear them boasting.

"My fangs are longer than yours!" said Rip.

"No they're not," said Tear.

"Let's ask Viktor to show us his!" said Gash.

"My mum told me not to show off," said Viktor through tightly-clenched teeth.

"Not through yet! Backward are we?" they laughed.

He sighed as he sat half-listening to what his mother was telling Dr. Pearce.

If only, he thought, I had someone like Margaret I could talk to it wouldn't matter so much if the others laughed at me.

Dr. Pearce shook her head as she read Viktor's thoughts.

"You see," she said to Evilina, "in order to develop properly, young vimps need a mixture of the blood collected by each of their parents. Of course, as you can't leave Viktor alone to collect it fresh, I expect you get your blood from the supermarket, don't you?"

Evilina nodded, "Yes. I order it on-line from Veinsbury's and it comes frozen in packs. All I have to do is heat it up."

"Mm," said Dr. Pearce. "Not terribly sure about supermarket blood. You don't know where it comes from. It could be contaminated or contain additives. And as for that stuff they claim is 'blue' – it's best avoided. But I suppose you've no alternative.

"Look. Why not take up Mr. Sharpe's offer of a bridge? It'll make things easier for him at school if he looks and feels like a vimp of his age and it's important for him to go on his First Flight with the rest of his class. And after his First Bite I think you'll find the problem will sort itself out."

She took a piece of silver birch bark and, dipping the talon of her forefinger into a jar of sooty liquid on her desk, scratched some words on it. She handed it to Evilina saying,

"Take this to the pharmacy next-door and they'll give you something to stop him being sick – just dab it on his tongue after his morning transfusion."

"Oh thank you, doctor!" said Evilina, smiling as

14

she took the prescription. But when she examined it outside it seemed to be splattered with crushed black spiders.

"She must be a very clever doctor," she murmured to Viktor as they walked towards the pharmacy, "because I can't read a word she's written."

# CHAPTER 4

Inside the pharmacy the place looked deserted. Curtains of cobwebs hung from the ceiling and there was a large pile of rags in one corner. A rickety shelf sagged under the weight of two huge tomes, the gold lettering of their titles gleamed through the gloaming: 'Spellbinding' and 'Potent Potions'. On another shelf grey, black and brown liquids swirled around in dusty medicine bottles as if they were trying to escape. And the counter top was covered with open dishes of pills.

Viktor read some of the labels, "Fighting Pills…Sleeping Pills…They all look the same," he said to Evilina.

"They may *look* the same but the effects are very different," said a squeaky voice from the corner.

The pile of rags rose up and Viktor and Evilina saw a shadowy figure whose face was almost hidden by long untidy hair. As she shuffled towards them she nearly tripped on the hem of her skirt, which swept the floor around her, but she managed to save herself by clutching a three-legged stool.

"What do you want?" she asked, peering at them through her veil of hair.

"Dr. Pearce would like you to make this up for my vimp Viktor," said Evilina, handing over the prescription. "He seems slightly allergic to blood at the moment."

"Hee! Hee!" the strange figure cackled. "Don't you remember me, Evilina? We were at school together. I'm Drakilly," she said as she took the prescription into a small room at the back of the pharmacy.

"DraSILLY! Silly-Dilly we called her," said Evilina to Viktor. "The most stupid vimp in our class! She never listened properly and always got everything muddled up – especially spelling. And so clumsy too! However did she become a pharmacist?"

"I didn't," said Dilly, coming back to the counter. "My cousin Distilly's the pharmacist. I'm only looking after the place because she's not well. We both fell ill while brewing medicines. But I'm better now."

"How do you manage to make up the prescriptions?" asked Evilina.

"Easy," said Dilly. "All I have to do is match the signs on the prescription with those on the bottles. Anyway, I remember collecting the herbs for this one with my cousin in the churchyard at midnight."

"Herbs!" exclaimed Evilina. "My vimp's not taking herbs!"

"Well, you said he's allergic to blood so maybe he's a vegetarian."

Vegetarian! Viktor thought. Vegetarian! Just like Margaret. That's why those raspberries looked so delicious. She liked them and so would I. If only we could meet we'd have lots to talk about.

"I said he might be a vegetarian," repeated Dilly. "My cousin told me about them."

"I know about vegetarianism!" said Evilina, "and I can spell it too which is more than you can, I'm sure. But my vimp is NOT a vegetarian. As I told you, he's just slightly allergic to blood at the moment."

"Don't know why you're getting so cross," said Dilly. "My cousin says there's nothing wrong with being different from everyone else.

"Now," she added, holding up a bottle of bright green liquid that reminded Viktor of the green vegetables he'd seen in gardening programmes, "do you want this medicine or don't you?"

"It looks a most unhealthy colour," said Evilina.

"Here," said Dilly to Viktor, "you take it."

But, as she handed the bottle over the counter, the cork popped out.

"Oops! How did that happen?" said Dilly as a stream of green liquid flowed over the pharmacy floor, turning it into a grassy meadow with sweet-smelling flowers.

Smells great, thought Viktor, sniffing it. But

Evilina held her nose, saying, "Ugh! It's a mos' disgusti'g sme'!"

The grass and flowers disappeared when Dilly went into the back room again. She brought out another bottle which she managed to place safely in Viktor's hands but, as she did, her sleeve caught the dishes on the counter and sent them flying.

"Oops! Can't think how that happened!" she said.

"She hasn't changed!" said Evilina to Viktor as they left the pharmacy with Dilly still scrabbling about on the floor trying to pick up the dusty pills. "Let's call into Mr. Sharpe's on our way home."

"Thought I'd see you again so I got this ready – lucky I took an impression of his upper jaw last time you came," said Mr. Sharpe, holding up a neat bridge with two tiny fangs.

"Why are the fangs so small?" asked Viktor, as Mr. Sharpe fitted it into his mouth.

"Best make them look as if they're developing naturally. If you arrived at school with a full-sized pair everyone would know they were false. In a month's time I'll change these for the next size up."

The following morning, the moment she'd dabbed Viktor's tongue with the medicine, Evilina fainted.

"I feel so weak!" she gasped as she came round. "I must go back to bed."

She was ill for the whole week of Viktor's half-term though she got up every morning to give him his transfusion and dab his tongue with the medicine. It seemed to work for he stopped being sick and, with Evilina out of the way, he was able to watch all the gardening, cookery and nature programmes on television he wanted without her interrupting him.

Wonder if Margaret is watching any of these? he thought.

And, rather than dreading going back to school, he was really looking forward to it. He kept pressing his thumbs against the two tiny points in his mouth,

"Now I'm like the others," he said to himself, "they'll all want to be friends with me!"

# CRAPTER 5

Evilina was still feeling ill when Viktor went back after half-term.

"I always seem to feel worse after I've given you your transfusion," she said, slumped in an armchair as he left.

Viktor hurried along the main tunnel to his school which was housed in the cellars and dungeons of an old castle. He arrived early and went round, grinning at everyone in the playground. But, by the time the bell went, no-one had noticed his fangs and he was restless all through the first lessons.

The time of his class's First Flight was drawing near and Ms Form, their teacher, was making sure that they were well prepared for it.

Ms Form was strict but great fun. Like all vampires she wore black clothes but hers were things she'd bought on the High Street in the human world: mini-skirts, thigh-high boots and leather bomber jackets. She also brought back recordings of the latest pop songs, teaching them the words and showing them how to disco dance.

"The kids up there love these things," she said, "and they'll think you're very weird if you don't know about them.

"Now, today I want you to practise being in a burger bar again. You can use some of the plastic cutlery and empty ketchup bottles I've brought in to help you. Get into groups and in ten minutes I'll come round to see how you're getting on. I'll be looking at what you order for your meal and how well you pretend to eat and drink. And I'll be asking how you plan to get rid of the food without arousing the humans' suspicion."

As usual, no-one wanted Viktor in their group so he had to pretend by himself in a corner of the classroom.

Ms Form had shown them so many pictures of burger bars he knew exactly what they were like. He imagined being in one with Margaret.

"What are you going to have, Margaret?" he said.

"Cheese-burger, I think. How about you?"

"I think I'll have a veggie-burger. Shall we have some cokes? Mm…This tastes good! Would you like some ketchup?" he said, turning the plastic bottle upside down and squeezing it in the way Ms Form had shown them.

"Do try to sound a bit more enthusiastic when you order, Rip. Remember you're meant to be hungry… What did I hear you say Tear?" said Ms Form.

# Viktor the Vegetarian Vampire

"Would you pass me the salt, please?" said Tear.

"What have I told you, Tear? Human children – kids – just like you vimps think it's very uncool to be polite to each other. Much better to shout, 'Giss the salt!' or reach across and grab it. And if ever you are stuck for what to say, remember those useful passwords I taught you: 'Yeah', 'Right' and 'Wha'ever'…Viktor, what have you ordered?" she asked, looking across the room to where he sat alone.

"A veggie-burger, Ms Form."

The rest of the class giggled and someone whispered, "Wimp!"

"Well, it's quite soft. There's no need to chew so hard – and don't forget the swallowing movement in your throat…No, Gash, you can't keep going to the loo to flush away bits of the meal. Someone's sure to notice. Slip it into a plastic bag. Remember, vimps, always carry a few plastic bags in your pocket. Then you can throw the food into the nearest litter-bin."

Break-time came at last. Viktor saw that Rip, Tear and Gash were on their usual bench in the playground so he went and stood near them. He hoped that, once they'd noticed his fangs, they'd ask him to join them.

"Why are you hanging around us, Fang-less?" growled Rip. "Push off now!"

Viktor opened his mouth wide and laughed as if Rip had made a good joke.

"Wait a minute," said Tear. "I believe our little Vikkums has something to show us. Trying to get us to see his point – or points!"

"Not very big, are they? Anyone got a magnifying glass? Ha! Ha!" said Gash, pushing his face right up to Viktor's mouth. But immediately he fell to the ground gasping, "Help me! Oh, help me! I feel ill!"

The others laughed, thinking Gash was pretending to faint at the sight of Viktor's tiny fangs. But when they saw he really was ill they rushed in to get Ms Form.

"Pull yourself together, Gash. You were perfectly alright before break. If you think you can get out of the written test by behaving like this you're wrong!" she said, dragging him back into the classroom. And, as it was the end of break-time, the others followed them.

"Now," said Ms Form, taking no notice of Gash who had flopped over his desk, "I'm going to test you on your half-term homework – the horror film; programmes on sport and pop music; the computer games you played and the texts you sent. All of these things will help you when you chat to the children you'll soon meet. Viktor, please give out these test papers."

Viktor collected the pile of papers. He knew that none of the programmes he'd watched would help him answer the questions so he went very slowly, stopping at each vimp's desk and saying, "That's yours," as he placed a test paper on the desk.

But every vimp he spoke to fell down, moaning, until the whole class was rolling around on the floor crying and waving their arms.

"Stop this nonsense at once!" said Ms Form. "And get down to work! Viktor bring me those left-over papers."

As he put them on her desk she leaned towards him saying, "You seem to be the only one behaving..." But she broke off, screaming as she fell to the floor, "Get away from me!"

Viktor stared at her. When the vimps had fallen down he thought they were trying to get out of doing the test. But when Ms Form fell and shouted at him he was so frightened that he ran home.

He found Evilina in bed watching one of her favourite hospital dramas: 'Emergency Ward'. He tried to explain what had happened.

"It's as if my breath is poisonous," he sobbed.

"What did you say? That's it! I'm sure it's your medicine – anything Dilly touches is bound to cause trouble! Bring me the bottle!"

Viktor took it out of the bedside cupboard and gave it to her. She uncorked it, took a quick sniff and fell back, gasping, onto her pillows.

"It can't be! Not even Dilly could be so stupid! It's

g…it's gar…it's GARLIC! Wait till I get hold of her! I'll have to phone – I don't feel well enough to go the pharmacy.…

"Hello…Dilly?…It's me…Evilina. I'm calling about Viktor's medicine. Do you remember what herbs went into it?"

Viktor was near enough to the phone to hear Dilly's voice reciting a long list.

"Now, Dilly, listen carefully. Was there any wild garlic in the graveyard? It's got a green stalk with a white flower on top…Oh, there were…And your cousin pointed to them and said, 'Some of those.' Are you sure?…Oh, your cousin's back…Let me speak to her.

"Ah, good morning, Distilly. Evilina Vicious here. I was just asking your cousin about the wild garlic…Oh!…You pointed to them and said, '*None* of those.'…Yes, yes. I know. She never listens carefully enough…You will? Oh, thank you.

"She's sending Dilly round now with some medicine made from herbs collected without Dilly's help," Evilina told Viktor.

Very soon they heard Dilly banging on the door.

"I'm all at sevens and eights today," she babbled as she came into Evilina's bedroom. She handed her a new bottle of medicine and went on,

"My cousin's better now but she's not a bit grateful for all my help. She said the place looked like a tip so I've got to hurry back to clean it up. Don't worry, I'll see myself out."

Seconds after she'd left the room they heard a loud bump and, when Viktor looked over the banisters, he saw Dilly in a heap at the bottom of the stairs.

"My foot must have caught in the hem of my skirt!" she called up to him as she left the house. She banged the front door so hard that the marble cherubs Evilina had brought back from the graveyard fell off the mantelpiece and broke.

"I was wrong," said Evilina. "I said she hadn't changed. She has. She's much, much worse than she was!"

Even though she recovered quickly Evilina was still worried about Viktor.

"We must go to see Dr, Pearce again," she said. "What I can't understand is why you weren't affected by the garlic like the rest of us!"

# CHAPTER 6

"It's all part of his condition," said Dr. Pearce, when Evilina and Viktor went to her surgery the next day. "As I said, I believe things will clear up after his First Bite."

She laughed when she heard the whole story.

"My surgery was full of worried parents and their vimps," she said. "I never thought my medicine would have such an effect. But then I didn't know garlic would be added to the herbs I prescribed! I think, Viktor, you'll find things very different at school from now on."

When Viktor went back he noticed the other vimps in his class seemed frightened of him and kept well away. But to the younger vimps, who'd also been pushed around by Rip and his gang, he was a hero. They'd seen Gash fall down and had heard what happened on the day of the test. They crowded round Viktor in the playground and some of the stronger ones hoisted him onto their shoulders, marching with him to where Rip, Tear and Gash were sitting.

"Why isn't Viktor the Victorious in your skullball team?" they said. "No wonder you lose all your matches. Don't expect us to keep coming to cheer you on. Just think how stupid you'll feel arriving for an away game without any supporters!"

The three looked at each other and then at the younger vimps crowding round them.

"Er," said Rip. "We were just saying that Spike's useless in goal. Always lets the skull in. Wonder if you'd like to be our goalie, Viktor?"

"School's great," Viktor told Evilina a few weeks later. "We won the last skullball match 100-0 because I didn't let in a single goal. You should have heard the cheering. And Rip, Tear and Gash are so pleased they're going to take up my idea of our training the younger ones at break-time."

"I am glad," said Evilina, smiling in a way he'd never seen before. "All we have to do now is go to Mr. Sharpe every month to have your fangs lengthened."

"Normally," explained Mr. Sharpe, "we can shrink or expand our fangs when we want. Obviously near humans we shrink them so we can close our mouths or they'd get suspicious and we only expand them when we're about to bite. I've made yours so you can flick them sideways with your tongue. They'll lie comfortably along the gum-line under your top lip until you want to bite. Then another flick of your tongue will bring them down."

29

Viktor practised each evening till his tongue was tired. He'd forgotten about wanting to be friends with human beings. For a time he'd even forgotten about Margaret. All he could think about was his First Flight on the fifth of November.

The date had been chosen by the Council of Vampires as the best one for the vimps' First Flight and First Bite. Each vampire family would attend a different bonfire party and, in all the bustle and excitement, pass unnoticed.

Evilina, like the other parents of vimps making their First Flight, had chosen a human family as 'blood' relations for the occasion. As Viktor had become so popular he was always being invited for sleepovers so she'd been free to visit the human world to make her choice.

"I met Jill Morgan," she told Viktor, "at a parents' evening at Castle School – quite near the graveyard. It's so important to choose the right family. At first it was rather difficult. Everyone seemed to know each other and people were talking in groups. Then I saw Jill standing alone in a corner of the room. I went over to her and began chatting – she seemed pleased to have someone to talk to."

"What did you say?"

"Oh, I told her we were hoping to move into the area soon and that I was looking at houses and schools. We hit it off straight away. Like me she's on her own. She said her husband Tom died from a sudden heart attack and I told her I'd lost mine that way too."

The next time she visited the Morgans Viktor had a great time at a sleepover in Rip's house, talking and laughing till way past midnight. When Evilina picked him up the following morning she was able to tell him more about his 'blood' relations.

"Though they've lived in the district for some time they've very few friends."

"How many children?" asked Viktor.

"Two. A boy, Bob, who's ten. He's been in hospital a long time. Jill said there's something wrong with his blood. He has to have transfusions. I told her you have them regularly and they're doing you a lot of good…And there's a girl. A teenager I think. Looks young for her age."

"What's her name?" asked Viktor.

"Jill did tell me. Now what was it? Piggy… Peggy…Meggy. Oh, I don't know. Some stupid human nickname."

"What's she like?"

"Quiet," said Evilina.

Quiet? thought Viktor. That's not much help. I need to know what she's like so I can think of the right things to say when we meet.

"Now," said Evilina, "it's important you don't make any mistakes so listen carefully. You're Vic and I'm

Evie Vince. I told Jill that since your dad died we've lived abroad."

"Where?"

"I said Romania. It's not a popular tourist spot so most people won't know much about it. We should be able to avoid any awkward questions. I told Jill we came back to the UK a few months ago and that we're living in Heyton – that's a village about ten miles from the town, Vamp-on-the-Hill, where the Morgans live."

Even with all the talk about the Morgans Viktor couldn't quite believe his First Flight was so near till Evilina took some clothes from a large bag.

"I bought these at a charity shop," she said, "so they look as if they've been worn. People would notice if you turned up to a bonfire party in new clothes."

Viktor chose some ripped jeans, a green sweatshirt and a red bobble hat that reminded him of a raspberry. There was also a pair of designer trainers he wanted to wear.

"They're great," said Evilina. "Couldn't resist them. They were such a bargain but you'd better wear these old wellies because it might be wet."

Then, from another bag, she brought out a black anorak with a huge white bat across the back.

"It feels strange," said Viktor, stroking the bat.

"You'll see why later," said Evilina. "It was plain

black when I bought it but I got Skilly the Wing-maker to put the bat on for me."

Viktor was trembling with excitement as Evilina helped him to put on the clothes.

"What do I look like?" he asked.

Evilina didn't reply but placed a shiny metal tray on its edge and leaned it against the wall.

"Look at this," she said. "What can you see?"

Viktor peered at it. "Nothing special," he said. "It's just a tray."

Evilina breathed a sigh of relief. "Thank Badness! No reflection. He's normal like the rest of us," she muttered to herself. She put on the bobble hat and anorak.

"There," she said. "This'll give you some idea."

"Wow!" said Viktor. "I'll look great. Just like a human kid."

"That's why I chose them. You'll put them on every day after school and then we'll practise the sort of things you'll say when we meet the Morgans.

"It'll be a busy time for you. I remember when I was a vimp there was so much to be done in the last weeks before our First Flight."

# CHAPTER 7

**M**um's right, thought Viktor as Ms Form kept them hard at work with loads of revision, testing and last-minute lessons.

One morning she pinned up two maps: one labelled Vampsville, the other Vamp-on the-Hill.

"Notice anything thing unusual about these maps?" she asked.

The class looked at them for a few minutes. Viktor put up his hand.

"They both look the same," he said.

"In a way they are," said Ms Form. "Our tombs are in St. Chad's churchyard which is on the outskirts of Vamp-on-the-Hill. Even though you've never been there, you won't get lost when you emerge for your First Flight because, as you can see, everything is arranged as it is here. Their main street is above our main tunnel and the shops, supermarket, health centre and pharmacy are exactly above ours. So is their school which is called Castle School because it was built where a castle once stood. You've all seen, in the corner of our playground, a flight of stone steps leading up to a large iron door, haven't you? Sometimes, if you listen carefully there, you can hear the shouts of the human children in their playground."

"O-o-oh" squealed the vimps.

Gash put up his hand. "When we leave for our First Flight, Ms Form, will we be going through that door?"

"No, Gash. That doorway is blocked by earth and stones from the castle which was pulled down a long time ago."

The moment the bell went for break-time all the vimps rushed to the steps to listen at the iron door but they heard nothing.

"Not surprised," said Ms Form when they told her. "It's the human children's half-term. Now, settle down for your Text-ing Test. Got your mobiles ready everyone?"

By the fourth of November all but one of the tests were over. That morning Ms Form said,

"Today we come to your final and most important test. It's a sort of dress rehearsal for your First Bite."

She took something that looked like a pile of coloured plastic from a black box. Handing Viktor a pump, she said,

"Choose two friends to help you pump this up."

Viktor chose Rip and Tear and, as they took it in turns to pump, a human figure, wearing jeans and a dark sweatshirt, took shape. When it was inflated Ms Form placed it in a lying-down position on a table and covered it with a sheet.

"Now," she said. "Each of you will go to the classroom door, open it, creep up to this figure, pull back the sheet and touch its neck with your mouth *closed.* You will then creep back to the door. And I shall time you."

Everything went well until it was Gash's turn. He was angry Viktor hadn't chosen him to help with the pumping so he opened the door carelessly, banged it shut and marched noisily towards the figure.

"Gash! Don't be stupid!" said Ms Form. "This is your last chance to practise the most important action that will turn you into a Full-Blooded Vampire.

"If you behave like that on your First Flight you'll be the only one who doesn't get his First Bite. Imagine how you'll feel then."

Gash did it again – this time perfectly.

"That's more like it!" said Ms Form. "Is that everyone? No. Viktor you've not had your turn yet. You're the last."

Viktor crept silently towards the figure but, as he leaned over it, his tongue accidentally flicked down his full-sized fangs which pierced its neck. It collapsed with a great who-o-shing sound while the rest of the class collapsed laughing round it.

"Good old Viktor!" gasped Rip.

"You'll have to stay behind, Viktor," said Ms Form, "to help me mend it."

As they patched up the figure's neck she said,

"I can't say I'm pleased about this but it proves that I was right to tell Mr. Fear you were ready to join the others for your First Flight. Your fangs are working well and we've heard no more from you about eating and wanting to make friends with human beings.

"I hope you and the others will enjoy the disco I've arranged to celebrate you all passing your tests."

That evening the vimps gathered in the main assembly hall which was decorated with small red lamps shaped like drops of blood.

"Phwoah!" said Rip. "Look at Ms Form!"

They all stared at her wonderful black gear: a mini-dress covered with spangles, long jet earrings, lacy tights and very high heeled shoes.

Viktor noticed her bright red lipstick and remembered Margaret's big red mouth and the raspberries. He'd been so busy and happy at school that he hadn't thought about her for a while.

It'd be great if she was here, he thought. Wonder if she likes discos? Don't suppose I'll ever get to meet her to find out.

"Now then, you've all worked hard so I want you to enjoy your last hours of being vimps!" said Ms Form.

And they did! The walls of the old dungeon echoed to the sound of them stamping and laughing and ducking under flashing laser beams.

Ms Form was a brilliant DJ, chatting, joking and keeping the music flowing.

"Anyone going to show us some break-dancing?" she said and soon they were all whirling round on their hands till the floor looked as if it was covered with black spinning tops.

But, at last, she said, "That's all folks! You need to have a good night's rest to be ready for your First Flight. By this time tomorrow you won't be vimps any more but Full-Blooded Vampires!"

# CHAPTER 8

On the afternoon of the fifth of November the vimps and their parents gathered in the school playground but Viktor and Evilina were nowhere to be seen. Ms Form went from group to group asking,

"Has anyone seen Viktor and his mother?"

"Probably scared now the time's come to do it for real," said Gash. He was still angry that, though Viktor's practice First Bite had gone wrong, Ms Form hadn't made *him* do it again.

"There's Viktor now!" shouted Rip.

"Where have you been?" asked Tear.

Viktor didn't answer. It had been a difficult morning both for him and Evilina. They'd overslept and it was gone midday by the time they woke up.

"I was so busy getting things ready I must have forgotten to set the alarm," said Evilina. "Oh, why's it taking so long for this blood to heat up?

"There!" she said, dabbing medicine on his tongue after his transfusion. "Thank Badness it's the last time I'll have to do that! By tomorrow morning

39

you'll be a Full-Blooded Vampire. Now go and get dressed."

Viktor went into his bedroom. Though he'd practised putting on human clothes everything seemed to go wrong: the zip of his jeans stuck, he put the sweatshirt on back to front and once his socks were on he couldn't find his wellies.

"Mum!" he called. "Have you seen my wellies?"

Evilina rushed into his room.

"You must know where you put them," she said. "If this is a trick so you can wear those trainers, forget it…Here they are! Under the clothes you took off and left on the floor after the disco last night."

Yet, even though they were late, Evilina said they needed to call in at the pharmacy and there were several customers ahead of them so they had to wait a long time. When, at last, it was their turn Viktor saw Distilly take a pill from the dish marked 'Sleeping Pills'. She put it in a small black envelope before giving it to Evilina, saying,

"There! That's double strength. Even Dilly managed her First Bite with the help of one of these."

"You'll have no trouble from Meggy tonight," Evilina told him as they hurried on to school.

They found the normally noisy playground hushed with both the vimps and their parents too nervous to say very much. Groups of younger vimps had come with their pet wolfhounds to watch but even they were silent, overcome by such a solemn occasion.

Ms Form was standing by her class.

"Not long now," she said, looking at her watch. "Clocks went back an hour last week in the human world so it'll soon be dark up there."

At last, after a long wait, there was a whisper, "He's coming!" and the crowd parted to allow Mr. Fear, his black gown swishing round him, to walk from the school and step onto a platform that had been put up at one end of the playground.

With his grey-green hair bristling under his mortar board and his bushy eyebrows that met together over his beaky nose, he looked very fierce. But when he spoke his gruff voice was kindly.

"My dear young vimps, for the past fifty years you have studied hard. Now the time has come to put into practice all you have learned. I'm sure you've been taught about the risks of eating, drinking, garlic, mirrors and the first light of dawn and that you have learned how to avoid these dangers.

"All that remains is for me to wish you well on your First Flight. Remember, you leave with your parents as vimps but, after your First Bite, you will return as Full-Blooded Vampires!"

At these words the choir of younger vimps stepped forward and, with Ms Form as conductor, sang the song Mr. Fear had composed hundreds of years before:

>*Jolly biting weather*
>*Be with you all tonight.*
>*Up, up together*
>*Soaring in your First Flight!*
>*May you overcome whatever*
>*Is in the way of your First Bite...*

The last two lines should have been repeated but the vimps had felt the song was old-fashioned and they'd persuaded Ms Form to let them add their own rap.

Leaning forward and swaying slightly they chanted

>*Dig that fang, vimp.*
>*Dig it deep.*
>*They won't stir –*
>*They're still asleep.*
>*Then the blood will flow until*
>*You drink your fill, vimp,*
>*Drink your fill*
>*Of blood, blood, blood,*
>*Blood, blood, blood!*

As the rap was finishing a huge black and silver escalator rose from the centre of the playground. Each vimp, with a parent on either side, stepped on to it. Viktor, clutching Evilina's hand, was the last. They moved slowly upwards with the howling of wolfhounds and chanting of 'Blood, blood, blood!' growing fainter and fainter behind them.

"This is ours," said Evilina when they got to the top. They stepped into a marble tomb and when she clapped her hands the slab on top flew open. She clambered out and turned to help Viktor over the steep sides.

"Here we are," she said. "At long last!"

# CHAPTER 9

The first thing Viktor noticed was the air. It was cool, clean and clear. But after several gulps he sat down, resting his back against the ivy which half-covered their tomb.

"I feel giddy," he said.

"It's the fresh air," said Evilina. "You'll soon get used to it. You have to breathe in a different way here. Breathe in 2. 3. Hold your breath 2. 3. And let it out 2. 3. Now practise that for a while. In 2. 3…"

Viktor sat on the ground with dry leaves rustling around him. It took him some time to get his breathing right but at last he felt steadier. He looked about him at the strange new world he'd heard so much about and waited so long to visit. There were only a few stars in the sky but vampires don't need light to see. He stared at the other graves with their marble urns and angels and read some of the inscriptions.

"Is that Rip's tomb?" he asked, pointing to one near theirs.

"No, silly. Didn't Ms Form teach you about R.I.P.? Mr. Fear told us it was Latin for 'Rest in Peace' – not that *we* ever get much rest. Do you feel better now? Sure? Jill told me to be there by six. We must make a start.

"Stand up and turn round," said Evilina, stroking the white bat on his anorak. Viktor felt the anorak getting tighter and tighter till it seemed to become part of his body like an extra layer of skin.

"There," said Evilina, waving her arms up and down.

Viktor watched as the two loose folds on the back of her jacket rose and stiffened into wings.

For a moment he wondered how he'd manage to fly. At school they'd all talked a great deal about their First Flight but Ms Form had never said anything about the actual flying. And they hadn't done any practice exercises for it as they had for being in a burger bar or their First Bite.

"Now," said Evilina. "Hold my hand!"

Up, up and up they soared and soon they were flying over the fields. Viktor almost forgot to breathe. He found he could flap the bat's wings and control his movements. After a while he said, "It's dead easy! Can I try by myself?"

"Just for a bit"

He swooped up and down, looping loops and squeaking, "Whee-e-e! Whee-e-e!"

In all his hundred years he'd never been as excited and happy. It was all so very different from

Vampsville, with its dark tunnels and low ceilings of earth, where everything was so cramped. This was a world with loads of space! Again and again he went up and dived down, enjoying the feeling of air rushing past him.

"Look at me, Mum!" he called up to her, turning a triple somersault before diving low over the twinkling lights of Vamp-on-the-Hill. It was exactly like the map Ms Form had shown them. There was the main street running right through the town, with Castle School near St. Chad's churchyard, and there was a big supermarket with its name in large orange letters – but what was that? A spelling mistake!

He felt Evilina would be pleased he'd spotted it. He zoomed up to her.

"Mum! Look!" he said pointing to the letters. "They've spelled Veinsbury wrong! They've put S.A. instead of V.E. at the beginning."

"The name is different in the human world," said Evilina. "Now, we'll soon be at the football pitch where the bonfire party is being held...Ah, there it is! We'd better go down behind that clump of trees."

As their feet touched the ground their wings folded back into their clothes and Viktor's anorak became looser till it felt less like a second skin and more like something he was wearing. He began to walk around, unsteadily at first because he'd never walked on grass before and it was springier than the hard earth he was used to in Vampsville. In the distance he could hear the sound of laughing and shouting.

"Try to remember everything we've practised, Viktor," said Evilina as they walked towards the sound.

"You mean Vic, don't you?"

"Well done, Vic! As I've told you, the most important thing is for you to get on with Meggy. Jill's very easy to talk to – she's so grateful for any attention – but I've never managed to get more than a few words from Meggy."

The sound of voices grew louder as they walked until they saw children running round a blazing bonfire with sparklers in their hands. Viktor stopped and stared.

"Don't be frightened," said Evilina. "I remember being scared when I saw my first human beings."

Viktor said nothing. He wasn't at all frightened – quite the opposite. He was completely calm and sure of himself in a way he'd never been before.

I can't believe that these are the strange creatures everyone's told me about, he thought. I've got a feeling I'll find real friends here.

"I'm O.K. Mum," he said. "We've practised this lots of times in school and I've got loads of things to talk about. I feel great! I just know everything's going to go well tonight!"

# CHAPTER 10

"**O**o-oo! Evie! Over here!" called a voice as they walked onto a muddy football pitch.

Evilina and Viktor went over to where a woman was putting out food on a long table.

"Hello Jill!" said Evilina. "Meet Vic. Like I told you, this is his first Guy Fawkes Night. They don't have it in Romania."

Viktor stared at his first human being. Jill was thin and had deep lines across her forehead. Her coat was unbuttoned and her long hair untidy. Standing next to Evilina, with her rosy make-up, smart black gear and hair tied back in a pony-tail, Jill seemed quite scruffy. But he liked her immediately. It was as if she was someone he'd known a long time.

"Great to meet you at last," said Viktor who'd been practising the words for weeks. "I've really been looking forward to it. Mum's told me so much about you."

"Nice to meet you Vic," said Jill. Then, turning to Evilina, she said, "I do hope things will be O.K. The other two who were going to help me dropped out at the last minute. And I don't know how Maggie and I will manage if everyone wants to be served at once."

"You're doing splendidly," said Evilina. "And there's no need for Meggy – I mean Maggie – now I'm here to help. I'm an old hand at this sort of thing."

"Good to have your support," said Jill. "Now, where's Maggie gone? I sent her to get some paper towels from Mollie Dixon who's giving out the toffee apples and gingerbread. Ah there she is. Maggie come over here!" she called across the field.

A small figure dressed in jeans, a yellow anorak and a striped woolly hat came towards them.

Viktor stared. He had the feeling he'd seen her somewhere before.

"Is it?…No, it can't be," he said to himself. Then, as the figure came nearer, he was sure. "Yes, it is!…It's Margaret!"

"Well, say hello to Vic!" said Jill.

"Hi!" said Maggie.

Viktor forgot what he'd meant to say. He could only look at her and mumble, "Mm…Yeah…Right… Wha'ever…I…I mean Hi!"

"I think everything is ready, dear," said Jill. "Why don't you and Vic grab some food and go to watch the fireworks? Evie'll help me here. What do you want, Vic, hot-dog or baked potato?"

"They both sound great," said Viktor.

"Maggie, baked potato or Quorn hot-dog? Don't know if I mentioned it, Evie, Maggie's vegetarian," said Jill.

"Why so's Vic! Quite a few kids are nowadays. It's good to think our young folk are growing up so thoughtful and caring," said Evilina, smiling at her.

Viktor stared at Evilina. She sounded so different from her usual sharp-tongued self – much more like a kind and loving mum.

I'll show you Mum, he thought, that I can do just as well!

"Could I have one of those delicious-looking potatoes, please?" he said.

Jill put butter and cheese into a large potato and handed it to him on a polystyrene tray saying, "Help yourself to tomato ketchup."

"He's a really nice kid," she said to Evilina. "Reminds me a bit of my Bob. You'll see when you meet him."

Viktor tipped the plastic bottle of ketchup upside down and squeezed on the bottom, just as he'd done with the empty bottle at school. But he squeezed so hard that ketchup spurted out all over the table. Evilina handed him a paper towel saying,

"Wipe it up with this, Vic dear." And she whispered, "Be careful, Viktor. Don't let any of it touch your lips."

After he'd finished mopping up he couldn't see a litter-bin anywhere so he stuffed the soggy towel into his pocket and walked with Maggie towards the bonfire. He wanted to talk to her about the television programme but he didn't know quite how to begin so he asked her some of the questions he'd practised with the others.

"What are the kids like at your school?"

"O.K.," she said.

"Are the teachers strict?"

"Not really."

"Is the work hard?"

"No," said Maggie.

He couldn't think what to say next so he began to break bits off his potato, bringing them to his mouth saying, "Mm. Delicious!" and then, with a flick of his wrist, throwing each piece into the bonfire.

"You know," said Maggie, "it's strange. I've never met you before but I'm sure I've heard your voice somewhere."

"I phoned in when you appeared on 'Down to Earth' on TV."

"Of course! You're Viktor from Gravesend! But your mum said you'd been living in Romania."

"Mm...I...We...We were visiting our family in Gravesend. They all live there."

He hoped she believed him and that she wouldn't ask any more awkward questions. He was relieved when a voice boomed over the loudspeaker,

"Ladies and gentlemen, boys and girls, may I have your attention please? The Firework Display is about to begin. Would you all go to the gate end of the pitch and take up your positions behind the line of white ropes. We don't want any accident to spoil a pleasant evening so please stay behind the ropes until the display is over."

Ms Form had taught them a great deal about Bonfire Night celebrations but Viktor had never imagined anything as wonderful as the fireworks that evening. He watched in amazement as they whirled and sparkled with jewel-bright colours, each one better than the last. Best of all, he thought, were the ones which opened out like flowers against the night sky but, instead of petals, they had hundreds of stars which changed colour as they fell to the ground.

He o-o-oed and a-a-ahed like the other children as they whizzed and fizzed but when there were loud bangs he thrust his fists into the pockets of his anorak and hunched his shoulders, hoping Maggie would think he was cold rather than frightened.

When it was all over they went back to the table where Jill and Evilina were clearing away.

"Mum said you've not seen fireworks before," said Maggie. "Did you like them?"

"Just awesome!" said Viktor. "I've never seen anything so fantastic! But it would have been better without the bangs…" he stopped, remembering how the others had laughed at him for being frightened of loud noises. But, to his surprise, Maggie said,

"That's what I think too but the others all laugh at me for being afraid."

"Maggie," said Jill. "Evie has been kind enough to say she'll stay with you while I pop in to see Bob. I haven't had time all day because of getting this stuff ready and I know he'll be feeling low because of missing the fireworks. Mrs. Miller from next-door is visiting her granny in the hospital and she's giving me a lift there and back…It's so good of you, Evie. Sure you don't mind?"

"What are friends for? I only wish I could come to the hospital with you," said Evilina, licking her lips.

# CHAPTER 11

"Now Maggie," said Jill, opening their front door, "make our guests feel at home." Then she ran back down the garden path to where Mrs. Miller was waiting in her car.

Evilina led the way into the kitchen as she'd been there before. But for Viktor it was the first time he'd been inside a human house.

It's not like those shiny-bright kitchens I've seen on TV adverts, he thought as he looked around. All those dirty dishes piled up in the sink!

"I'll do these," said Evilina, "Jill will be too tired when she gets home. You two go and watch telly."

"Must feed Bassy first, Aunt Evie," said Maggie.

"Now Maggie, remember what I said? You're almost grown up so call me Evie," said Evilina.

"O.K. Evie. It's just that I would like an auntie. We don't seem to have any relations like other people. Dad's brother Ben is in Australia but all we get is a card at Christmas," said Maggie, spooning some food onto a dish marked 'Bassy'.

"Funny. She doesn't seem hungry," she said as

the cat, hunching her back with her fur standing on end, looked hard at Viktor and Evilina. At last, she edged towards her dish still glaring at them. After filling Bassy's water bowl Maggie went with Viktor into the next room.

When they had settled down in two shabby but comfortable armchairs, Maggie said, "You know – there's something I don't understand. Your mum says you're vegetarian but when you phoned into 'Down to Earth' you didn't seem to know what being vegetarian meant."

Help! What do I say now? thought Viktor. Talking to Maggie here isn't the same as it was talking to her in my head. She was always friendly then. Now she seems to be trying to catch me out all the time.

"O-oh!" he said. "I...I decided to become a vegetarian after talking to you. It made me think."

"Do you mean I changed your mind? That's great!" she said. "What other TV programmes do you watch?"

"Things like cookery and nature programmes but I like the ones about gardening best, especially when they're about fruit and veg. Makes your mouth water."

Maggie laughed. "Yes, those raspberries were really great!"

She didn't speak for a few moments. Then she said, "It'll be good when you come to our school so I won't be the only one to enjoy things like that."

"What do you mean?" asked Viktor.

"Well...well...on my first day at the school we had to write about what we really wanted most. And I wrote about wanting an allotment so we could always have fresh fruit and veg. and Mr. Dennis read mine to the class. He said I wrote very well and it was nice to find someone my age who didn't want loads of money or to be a pop star celebrity."

"Wow!" said Viktor. "Bet you were pleased!"

Maggie didn't speak but her eyes filled with tears. Viktor wondered what to say. None of the conversations he'd practised in school had gone like this.

"I was when he said it but afterwards, at break-time, Bea Richmond and her gang all crowded round me asking why I hadn't chosen something like pop records, iplayers or holidays abroad. I said I liked fresh air and fresh food.

"And then Mr. Dennis sent my work to the gardening programme but being on television made it worse for me. Bea and her gang kept saying, 'You looked like a clown with that big red mouth!'

"Now they call me 'potato-face' and pull at my clothes saying, 'Been gardening in these?' But Mum hasn't got the money to buy me designer gear like theirs...and...it's not just the name-calling...no-one seems to want to play with me or invite me home."

"I know how you feel," said Viktor. "Something

like that happened to me once."

"Did it? What did you do?"

Viktor wished he hadn't said anything.

"Well...it was when we first went to Romania. I couldn't speak the language so I had to make signs and all the other children laughed and imitated me," he said, feeling pleased at inventing such a good story. "But once I could speak Romanian I became very popular."

"How?" asked Maggie.

Once again Viktor wished he hadn't said so much. He remembered only too well what had really happened.

Wonder how Rip and the others are getting on with their 'blood' relations? he thought.

"Oh, it changed gradually," he said. He didn't want to say anything else in case she asked more questions.

"Not watching telly?" asked Evilina, coming in with two steaming mugs on a tray. She put one in front of each of them. Maggie's was filled with foaming cocoa while Viktor's had only enough boiling water to make it steam.

"Drink that up and then, Maggie, it'll be time for bed. I promised Jill you'd be asleep by the time she came home."

"Mmm," said Maggie. "The cocoa tastes different from when Mum makes it – much nicer! Did you say you were coming again, Evie?"

"Yes, probably in a week or so's time. More houses to look at. But I told Jill I'd look after you whenever she wanted me to."

"I am rather tired," said Maggie when she'd finished her cocoa. "Night, Vic. Night-night, Evie."

Evilina listened as Maggie's footsteps on the stairs died away. She looked at the clock and then took the mugs back into the kitchen.

Viktor snuggled deeper into the armchair. He'd forgotten why they were there and almost believed they really were going to move to Vamp-on-the-Hill.

This is great, he thought. Even though she's different from how I thought she'd be, I really like Maggie. When I go to her school I'll be able to help her stand up to those horrid kids in the playground.

"Now Viktor!" said Evilina, coming back into the room, "the ten minutes have passed. She'll be fast asleep by now. So up you go!"

# CHAPTER 12

**V**iktor stared at her. "Wh-wh-what do you mean?" he stammered.

"I said she'll be fast asleep by now. I put a sleeping pill in her cocoa and it takes ten minutes to work so when you dig your fangs into her neck she'll be too sleepy to resist. Distilly said even Dilly managed her First Bite when her mum slipped one of these into the cocoa of her 'blood' relation."

In a flash Viktor remembered the real reason for their being in the Morgans' house and he stopped feeling comfortable and began to feel sick instead – as sick as he had after his transfusions. When they'd practised their First Bite in the classroom it had all seemed good fun. But he hadn't met Maggie then.

"I don't want to bite her," he said. "I like her."

"Don't be stupid," said Evilina. "You can't like her. She's a human being. Go upstairs immediately! You've no time to waste. Distilly told me that the pill took ten minutes to work but its effects only last for ten minutes."

59

Viktor didn't move.

"Go on!" said Evilina. "You know what Dr. Pearce said about all your problems clearing up after your First Bite? I can't keep giving you transfusions forever."

"I don't want to hurt Maggie."

"You won't hurt her," said Evilina. "Don't they teach you anything in school nowadays? Seems to me they're too busy trying to make learning fun. Forget all that nonsense you may have heard in the playground about turning her into a vampire – that sort of thing takes centuries of practice. And as for that rubbish in the young vimps' rap about 'drinking your fill' – the First Bite is different for everyone – sometimes your fangs go deep and sometimes they don't. All that's really necessary with your First Bite is for you to break her skin and lick a few drops of blood."

Viktor hesitated for a moment. If that was all he had to do and Maggie wouldn't be hurt and they could still be friends…then perhaps…But he realised almost immediately that was impossible.

"I can't do it," he said.

"Of course you can. If Dilly could do it so can you. And once you've tasted even a few drops of blood you'll feel very differently or, if you don't, you can live off blood from Veinsbury's like Dilly has done for years and I've done since I lost Vlad."

"But it's all human blood," said Viktor. "It has to come from somewhere or rather someone…"

"I don't know what's got into you!" said Evilina. "I used to worry that you were too quiet but ever since we arrived in the human world you've been full of yourself. Now, Jill will be back any minute so up you go! I'll wait for you at the bottom of the stairs. And don't worry. It won't hurt Maggie."

Viktor stood up and walked to the stairs. He climbed them as slowly as he could, wishing he could run back down and make a dash for the door. But every time he looked over his shoulder he saw Evilina standing on the first step, blocking his way and whispering, "Hurry up! There's only eight minutes left!"

His mouth and tongue were so dry he found it difficult to flick his fangs down and had to do it with his fingers. He opened the bedroom door and went in. His eyes glowed in the darkness as he looked round the room – there was a lamp on a little table beside a bed and a large wardrobe with mirrored doors.

He crept over to the bed, exactly as he'd practised in class, and gently pulled back the sheet. Maggie was lying on her front so all he saw was a mop of hair and her pyjamas with a pattern of pink roses. He tried to brush her hair away from her neck but she sprang up at once.

"Who is it?" she said, switching on the bedside light.

He was surprised at how quickly she'd woken up. He wanted to run downstairs but he knew Evilina would only send him back. What could he do? And what could he say to Maggie?

"Thought...you...might...like to play a game of...of...of Vampires. It's great fun! I've played it with my mates. Look!" he said, curling his lips back, "I've put in some false fangs. Now, you lie still and I'll pretend to bite you."

Maggie bounced out of bed. She didn't look like a mouse at that moment – more like a wild-cat.

"Sounds a stupid game!" she snapped. "Come anywhere near me with those false fangs and see what you get!"

And she hurled herself at him, scratching, biting and kicking. Viktor found it difficult to defend himself.

"Stop it, Maggie! Stop it! This isn't how you play the game...OW!...OW!...O-O-OW!"

He struggled hard to get away from her but she gripped him tightly. They rolled over and over on the floor but when they got to the wardrobe Maggie looked up and suddenly let him go. She sat on the floor, looking like a frightened mouse again, and stared at him. Viktor was rubbing his neck and crying.

The next minute Evilina burst into the bedroom.

"What's going on here? Maggie, get back to bed! Whatever will your mother say? Vic, come with me.

"Pull yourself together," she said as they went downstairs. "We'll have to make a run for it before Jill gets back".

But by the time they got to the foot of the stairs they heard a key turning in the lock and the front door opened.

As Jill walked in she came face-to-face with Evilina who stood in front of Viktor so that Jill wouldn't see he was crying.

"Bob O.K.?" asked Evilina.

"Yes, he's had a good day. Everything all right here?"

"Absolutely fine, Jill," said Evilina, pushing past her and dragging Viktor through the still-open door. "I'll give you a ring next week...Must fly now!"

# CHAPTER 13

When they'd flown over the fields earlier that evening Viktor had been excited because it was his First Flight and Evilina had been hopeful that his First Bite would solve all his problems – and hers.

But their journey back was very different. Evilina was snarling, "Just let me get my hands on her!" while Viktor was still crying when they arrived at their tomb.

"She bit me!" he wailed. "She dug her teeth into my neck!"

"Where?" said Evilina. "Let me see…Ah!…Thank Badness the skin's not broken."

Viktor stopped crying. "What would've happened if it was?" he said.

"Same as if you'd eaten. You'd have turned into a human being. Your father told me that, on your Aunt Bloodjilly's first visit to her 'blood' relations, she ate something and became human. And of course she could never return to our world. Terrible fate!" said Evilina, shuddering.

"Now stop crying. It wasn't *your* fault. Just wait till I get my hands on Dilly!"

"It wasn't Dilly. It was Maggie," he sniffed, fumbling in his pocket. He pulled out the paper towel, still soggy with ketchup.

"Aha!" said Evilina, pouncing on it. "We don't want anyone to know that you haven't had your First Bite." And she dabbed the ketchup onto his fangs and round his mouth.

As they went down the staircase from their tomb to their home she said,

"Let's stroll along the Main Tunnel. And if we see anyone give them a big smile so they can see the red on your fangs."

But, as they got back earlier than the others, they saw no-one except Dilly who was wandering round in her usual aimless way.

"Come home with us, Dilly," said Evilina. "There's something I want to tell you."

Dilly smiled – she almost never got invitations – but she stopped smiling when Evilina began shouting at her the moment they got inside the house.

"You vacant-minded vampire! Trust you to make a mess of everything! What did you do with the pills you spilled on the pharmacy floor?"

Dilly scratched her head. "What pills?"

"You remember. That time we came in to get Viktor's first prescription."

"Oh, *those*! I put them back in the dishes."

"But they were all mixed up," said Evilina. "Why didn't you sort them out?"

"I couldn't!" said Dilly. "They all looked the same!"

"So when I went to buy a Sleeping Pill from your cousin and she took one from a dish marked 'Sleeping Pills' it could have been a Fighting Pill?"

"S'pose so," muttered Dilly.

Ah! That's why Maggie changed from mouse to wild-cat, thought Viktor.

"Well, thanks to you," went on Evilina, "Viktor has missed the chance of his First Bite…Oh! What can I do now? If only Vlad was here to help me!"

"Do you want to talk to him?" asked Dilly.

"How can I, stupid? He's gone forever."

"You can still speak to him," said Dilly. "I read a spell about it in my cousin's book."

"No," said Evilina. "You've done enough damage with your cousin's pills."

"But this is a very good spell and very easy."

"No!" said Evilina. "Viktor and I are going to watch the next episode of 'Operating Theatre' to calm our nerves before we go to bed."

She switched on the television and settled down on the sofa which faced away from Dilly. "Come, Viktor," she said, patting the place beside her. Viktor wanted to watch Dilly casting the spell but Evilina pulled him onto the sofa near her.

"Now," said Dilly. "You spell out the name of the one you want to talk to...V...V...How do you spell Vlad, Evilina?"

"V.L.A.D." said Evilina, her eyes fixed to the screen where green-clothed figures in caps and gowns were gathered round a patient on the operating table.

"Oh thanks. V.A...A.."

"V.L.A.D." repeated Evilina, still gazing at the television.

"V.L.A.D." chanted Dilly, "V.L.A.D. Vlad Vicious come to me...O-Ooh!" she squealed. "My head's in a whirl and I can't think straight!"

"No change there, then," muttered Evilina as she went on watching the programme. "No spell is strong enough to knock sense into your thick head."

"I think it's working!" said Dilly. "I feel someone's sending a message to my brain."

"What brain?" snorted Evilina.

Viktor leaned sideways over the arm of the sofa, trying to see and hear what was going on though it was difficult because Evilina kept pulling him back, saying,

"Do sit still Viktor! How can I enjoy the programme with you wriggling about like that?"

But Viktor, craning his neck round, could see Dilly was surrounded by a swirling grey mist and that the faint outline of a figure was coming towards her.

"He's here! He's here!" cried Dilly. "My spell has worked! Oh! Oh! Hello…are…you…Vlad?"

Suddenly the picture on the screen was replaced by tiny black and white dots and a loud crackling drowned out the sound. Evilina was furious. "What's happening!" she shouted, pressing every button on the remote control. "The surgeon's just going to make his first cut!"

She's too busy to notice me, thought Viktor as he knelt up and peered over the back of the sofa to watch Dilly more closely.

He saw a stream of tiny bats flying from the figure and they seemed to be going towards Dilly's head.

"Oh," she said. "I can't hear you but I'm getting a feeling…that…you are not allowed to speak…but… if…I keep very still…I will understand what you want to say.

"I am being very still, Vlad. I am ready to receive your message…Ah…I'm allowed to…ask you…only one question…Oh dear! Only one!…What shall I ask him, Evilina?"

"Oh…Ask him what we should do," said Evilina thumping and kicking the set. "I'm missing all the best bits!"

"Wassat?" asked Dilly. "Didn't hear you. Did you say 'What happened to you?'?… Ah, he's answering…a…stake…through…the…What was that, Vlad? I didn't catch the last bit…Oh, he's gone!"

The picture and sound came back as suddenly as they had disappeared and Evilina settled deep into the sofa to watch every detail of the operation.

"Don't you want to know what he said?" asked Dilly.

Evilina didn't reply. She was staring at the screen, licking her lips.

"Be like that then. I know you don't believe my spells work. Well, tell me, if this one didn't, who was I speaking to? Myself? Oh, I do wish you'd joined in. You'd have remembered his last word: stake through the…?"

"Ah!" squealed Evilina. "He's cut through to the stomach!"

"The stomach!" echoed Dilly. "That could be it!"

She was still muttering to herself, "Stake-through-the-stomach, stake-through-the-stomach," when Viktor saw her to the door.

"Do you think she did see Dad?" he asked Evilina when the programme was over.

"Viktor Vicious! Do you think I would have gone on watching television if I thought there was the slightest chance of seeing your father again? I've known Dilly and her so-called spells since we were at school together. No-one wanted to play with her so she'd try to get our attention by saying she knew of a marvellous spell – she never did though.

"Now, bed. I'll phone Jill in a few days' time and offer to look after Maggie the next time she wants to visit Bob. And this time you really must get that First Bite!"

# CHAPTER 14

The next time they visited the Morgans, Viktor had a feeling that someone was following them down the street. Looking round, he saw an old beggar-woman, lurking in the shadows close behind them. He was just going to tell Evilina about it when they saw Jill and Maggie hurrying towards them.

"You told me, Evie, you'd like to visit Bob," said Jill, "so I thought you could come with me this evening."

"But what about the kids?" asked Evilina. "We can't leave them alone."

"I was coming to that," said Jill. "Bob's only allowed two visitors at a time. So I thought I'd treat the kids at the burger bar, next-door the hospital, while we visit Bob."

"Oh I don't know," said Evilina. "Such unhealthy food – full of saturated fat and additives."

"They've cleaned up their act a lot lately – cutting down on such things and serving wholemeal rolls and salads," said Jill.

"But would they be safe there?" said Evilina. "You hear stories about all sorts of strange folk hanging round such places."

"Don't fuss so," said Jill. "Liz – a friend of Mrs. Miller – works there and I'm sure she'll keep an eye on them for us...Look! There's our bus! We must run for it!"

They got on, panting, and found the bus very crowded.

"There are two seats inside, Jill," said Evilina. "You and Maggie take those. Vic and I will go upstairs. Up you go, Vic!"

Viktor went up, clutching the handrail as the bus lurched forward. He was scarcely able to believe his luck at the way things had turned out.

After what had happened the time before, Evilina wanted to make sure that Viktor's second attempt would go better. She'd allowed him to wear the designer trainers to boost his confidence and she'd asked Distilly to make up an extra strong Sleeping Pill.

"That should knock Maggie out after just a few sips of cocoa," she told Viktor. "No nonsense about her going upstairs and you waiting to follow. She'll fall asleep in the armchair and I'll be on hand to help you. Then one quick bite and we'll be away long before Jill comes home."

With her plan ruined, Evilina was fuming as she sat down beside him.

"There goes another chance of making your First Bite! Don't know what's got into Jill. She seems to have changed – much more assertive! Oh, well, I suppose we'll have to accept the situation for now. And I must say I *would* like to see the inside of a real hospital. But the very next time Jill visits Bob I'll make sure she goes alone."

Viktor didn't say anything. He was pleased he wouldn't have to bite Maggie that evening. Next time was some way off and anything could happen before then. He was enjoying his first bus-ride, watching the bustle of people shopping and stream of traffic on the busy streets. And he was looking forward to visiting a real burger bar.

As the bus slowed down Evilina said, "Now do be careful with all that food around! Got your plastic bags ready?"

"Yeah," said Viktor, patting his pocket. "Didn't use them for the baked potato. Don't worry. We've practised this!"

The bus stopped by some grand wrought-iron gates in front of a very large building.

"That's the hospital," said Jill, as they got off.

They walked a bit further till they came to the burger bar.

"Here we are," she said, leading the way.

Viktor looked round. It was exactly like the pictures Ms Form had shown them – plate glass, bright lights and lots of stainless steel. But there were no customers – only a man who seemed to be the manager. He was rather like a burger himself with a round pink face sandwiched between light brown hair and white tunic and trousers.

"Where's Liz?" asked Jill.

"You may well ask," said the man. "Began her shift quarter of an hour ago. Right as rain she was. There was only one customer in the place when, suddenly, Liz who was making up her order screamed and fell down in a dead faint. When she recovered she was so confused I had to send her home in a taxi."

"Oh dear! I am sorry," said Jill.

"Not easy to get staff at short notice," he went on, "so, when the customer offered to take Liz's place, I had to say 'Yes'. She says she's had some experience of serving."

"Where is she now?" asked Evilina.

"Downstairs, changing."

Evilina and Jill looked at each other. Then Jill said to the manager, "Look. My friend and I are going next door to visit my little boy who's sick in hospital. Could you keep an eye on these two? We won't be long."

"Don't worry," he said. "I'll see they don't come to any harm."

"Sit there," said Jill, pointing to a table for two by the window, "and be sure you stay there till we come to collect you."

"And whatever you do," added Evilina, "don't talk to any strangers. Remember Jill and I are only next-door. Got your mobile, Vic?"

Viktor nodded.

"Come on, Evie," said Jill and they hurried off.

As soon as they'd gone a great silence came over the place and all the lights went out.

"Mr. Biggs!" called a voice from below, "Mr. Biggs! The lights have fused!"

"You come up here!" he called. "Then I'll go down and fix them."

"Now," he said when the new assistant appeared, dressed in a red tunic with matching cap, "I told those kids' mums I'd look after them. We don't want them coming to the servery in the dark – they might slip. You go and get their orders then take the food to their table…Where did I put that torch?…Ah, here it is."

He switched it on and turned its powerful beam towards the containers in the servery. "Steak-burgers, hamburgers, cheeseburgers, veggie-burgers and chips," he said, pointing to each in turn. "Garlic bread's in that basket, salad's in that bowl, cokes are in the fridge."

"What's that?" asked the assistant, pointing into a dark corner.

"What?" he said, turning his torch to the corner. "My word! You've got sharp eyes. I didn't see that.

Seems to be a skateboard. Kids are always leaving things behind. Not in your way, is it?...You stay put," he said to Viktor and Maggie. "Our new crew-member will come to you...Everything's going wrong today. Good thing we cook on gas."

Viktor and Maggie heard him still grumbling as he went down the stairs.

"Look," said Maggie, as they waited for the new assistant to take their order. "I want to say I'm sorry I lost my temper the other night. Don't know what got into me."

Viktor could have told her but all he said was, "That's O.K. My fault really. I probably frightened you. I shouldn't have done it."

"I'm glad you did."

"Why?"

"Because it showed me I could stand up for myself if I wanted to. The next day I was by the drinking-fountain in the playground when Bea Richmond came up and tried to push me away."

"What did you do?"

"Squirted water right into her face. She turned bright red and shouted, 'What do you think you're doing?' And I said, 'I'm watering a big, fat, red tomato!' and everyone laughed. Bea burst into tears and ran into the girls' loos. And loads of people came up to me saying, 'Good for you! She had it coming to her!' "

"What are you two having?" asked the new assistant, coming over to their table.

"Shall we have veggie-burgers, Vic?" said Maggie.

"Yeah. With lots of chips, salad and cokes," he said, thinking it was a lot more fun ordering in a real burger bar than pretending in the classroom.

"Garlic bread?" asked the assistant, leaning over him.

Viktor hesitated. He looked up and saw it was Dilly, smiling at him under her smart peaked cap!

# CHAPTER 15

**V**ery soon she was back with their order.

"Enjoy!" she said, slamming two trays onto their table with such force that several chips fell on the floor.

"What about our cokes?" asked Viktor.

"Oops! Forgot about those!" said Dilly, going back to the servery.

Maggie took a large bite of her veggie-burger. "Great!" she mumbled with her mouth full. "I'm starving!"

Viktor slipped a plastic bag from his pocket onto his lap hoping that, in the semi-darkness, Maggie wouldn't notice when he put pieces of his burger into it. As he broke off a large chunk, he noticed Dilly looking at him and saw a swirling grey mist rising up around her. Then she began to chant:

"Ta-a-a-ake stea-ea-ea-eak

Ta-a-a-ake stea-ea-ea-eak

Take steak! Take steak!"

Viktor was transfixed, unable to take his eyes off her. Instead of slipping bits of the burger he was holding into the plastic bag, his arm moved like a robot's towards his open mouth. It was almost on his lips when Maggie cried out, "STOP! She's given you a STEAK not a veggie-burger! Can't you smell it?" she asked, wrinkling up her nose. "Let's get her to change it."

For a moment Viktor stared at her. He was still half-dazed but managed to say,

"No. It's O.K. I've got loads of chips and salad."

He forked a piece of tomato and was pretending to eat it when there was a clattering sound as Dilly arrived on the skateboard, coming to a halt just behind him.

"Your cokes!" she said. But, as she leaned over to put them on the table, the skateboard wobbled and she almost fell. Trying to keep her balance, her elbow dug sharply into Viktor's back. He gave a squeal of pain. And, as he lurched forward, the piece of tomato he was holding was nearly thrust into his open mouth.

"Sorry," said Dilly. "I almost fell. I'll get the hang of it soon!" And she rattled back to the servery.

"You O.K.?" said Maggie. "Have some coke."

"I'll be all right in a minute," said Viktor.

"Guess what?" said Maggie. "Mrs. Jones has asked us to share her allotment. She says it's getting too much for her to manage alone. Next time you come I'll take you over there and you can help me decide what to plant."

Viktor nodded and smiled. He wasn't really listening to her – he was listening to the voices in his head. There were two of them. One said,

"Wow! That's the second time in a few minutes that I've nearly had food in my mouth. Could have changed me into a human being! And I wouldn't have been able to go back to Vampsville. I'd have had to stay here like my Aunt Bloodjilly did."

"But," said the second voice, "that's exactly what I want to do! I enjoy human things like fireworks, riding on buses and chatting with a friend in a burger bar. If I stayed here I could go to school with Maggie and we could grow raspberries on the allotment.

"I don't want to bite Maggie – not now, not the next time, not ever. And I know I won't be able to bite anyone else either. So I'll never become a Full-Blooded Vampire – and I don't want to. All I want to do is to stay in the human world."

Viktor looked at the piece of tomato on his fork again but this time he saw it as something that could help rather than harm him.

Very slowly he raised his fork to his mouth and began to nibble. He chewed the skin and rolled the acid-sweet flesh around his mouth with his tongue. Delicious! Then he went on to the seeds in the jelly in the middle. Same taste but different textures.

As he ate a strange warm feeling was creeping up inside him. It began at his toes, moved to his legs and then spread through his whole body until it reached the top of his head and the tips of his fingers.

"What do you think we should plant?" asked Maggie.

"Oh…Yeah…Right…Wha'ever," gabbled Viktor, wriggling his warm toes inside his trainers.

He looked around him. It's like I'm waking from a dream, he thought. At home I've often dreamed of being in the human world. And now I am it's Vampsville that seems like a dream.

"You're very quiet," said Maggie. "Sure you're O.K.?"

He looked at her. She's so kind, he thought. She's a real friend – not like Rip and Tear. You can share secrets with friends you know won't let you down.

"There's something you need to know about me," he began and went on to tell her everything: about his being a vampire; his real troubles at school; his false fangs and First Flight and even about the Fighting Pill.

To his amazement she didn't scream or faint or do any of the things he'd been told human beings do when they recognise a vampire. She laughed and said, "That explains it!"

"What d'you mean?"

"After you'd gone the other night, I stopped being angry but I still couldn't get to sleep. I knew something wasn't quite right. Couldn't think what it was. And then I remembered. While we were fighting I caught sight of my reflection in the wardrobe mirror but yours wasn't there so I seemed to be fighting by myself."

"And you understood?"

"Oh yes," she said. "I got a book about vampires once from the library. Mum said I shouldn't be filling my head with such nonsense and made me take it back. But I Googled 'Vampires' on the library computer though it didn't tell me anything that surprised me. It's as if I knew everything all along. I used to imagine I had a vampire friend. Suppose it sounds stupid but I'd talk with him – not out loud, of course, but in my head – when things weren't going well at school then I didn't feel so alone."

"Weird!" said Viktor. "Because, after I'd talked to you on that phone-in, I imagined we were friends and I'd talked to you – in my head – and it made me feel better."

"Wish I could visit your world," said Maggie.

"It'd be too dangerous," said Viktor. "The others aren't like me. You wouldn't last long."

Suddenly the lights went on again. Dilly skated in their direction, waving her arms and saying,

"Whe-e-ee! I'm getting good at this"

She looked at Viktor's plate.

"Not hungry?" she said.

"The tomato was enough," he said.

"Ah," said Dilly. "It was a *beefsteak* tomato so I suppose that would work just as well."

She picked up their trays and moved in the direction of the servery but the skateboard skidded on the chips on the floor and she careered wildly between the tables. At the top of the stairs she let go of the trays. As they flew through the air Viktor's uneaten meal fell all over Mr. Biggs who was coming up.

"Who threw that?" he roared, with grease dripping off his face and shreds of lettuce in his hair he looked even more like a burger.

"Sorry sir!" said Dilly and then she burst out laughing and pointed to the lettuce. "Suits you! Get them to put green highlights in when you get your hair done!"

Mr. Biggs' pink face turned bright red.

"That's it!" he shouted. "First you fuse the lights so everyone thinks we're closed – we should be packed at this time of night. Then when I mended the fuse I found you'd left the tap on so I had to mop up and now I've had a faceful of food and an earful of lip! You're fired!"

"So are you!" said Dilly and, waving her arms,

she chanted, "Fire! Fire! Rise higher...higher!... Oops! I've forgotten how it goes on!"

At that moment Evilina rushed in and seized Viktor by the hand, saying to Maggie, "Stay put till your mum comes to collect you."

"I'll take the kid to her mum if you like," said Dilly.

"Fine!" said Evilina, scarcely looking at her. And, still clutching Viktor's hand, she hurried out.

"Keep hold of my hand, will you?" begged Viktor, when they got outside the burger bar. "I feel too tired to fly."

"Oh very well," said Evilina as they took off. "We'll have to fly lower tonight because I'm loaded with goodies."

But they were wafted higher by gusts of hot air. Looking down Viktor saw that the burger bar was ablaze. Great tongues of flames licked its walls and the smoke that spiralled up made him cough. On the pavement outside the burning building he saw Mr. Biggs jumping up and down, waving his arms. Then he saw Dilly on the skateboard, with Maggie behind clinging on to her, going through the hospital gates.

"Maggie's safe," he murmured. "Dilly's idea of firing is different from Mr. Biggs'," he said to Evilina.

But his words were drowned by the sound of clattering fire engines and the wail of police car sirens.

# CHAPTER 16

"We'll never be able to go back to the Morgan's again," said Evilina when they got home.

"Why not?" asked Viktor.

"It's a long story…It was boring in the ward – no blood anywhere. And Bob was boring too. So, after chatting to him for a bit, I told Jill I needed to go to the loo. But really I went to look for the Blood Bank because I'd noticed the signs when we came in. I soon found it and luckily a nurse was opening the door so I slipped in as she was fumbling with the light switch.

"What a wonderful sight it was! Racks and racks of plastic baskets filled with packages of blood! I was cramming as many as I could into my pockets when the nurse saw me and raised the alarm. I had to run along the corridor and fly from the nearest window." Evilina was putting the packages into their freezer as she spoke.

She hasn't asked me what happened in the burger bar, thought Viktor. Wish I was back there talking to Maggie. It was nice and warm. It's so cold down here.

"It's chilly, isn't it?" he said, shivering.

"No, it's not. What's wrong with you?" said Evilina, looking at him. "You're not ill, are you? I must say you look rather pink. Go to bed now. You'll feel better in the morning."

Viktor went to bed but he didn't get much sleep. He was so cold – at least on the outside though the warm feeling inside that he'd had in the burger bar was still there.

"Oh dear," said Evilina, getting his transfusion ready the next morning. "Your face is much pinker and your eyes look quite brown! A transfusion will soon put you right."

Viktor tore the tube from her hand and threw it in the bin. "I'm never going to have another transfusion!" he cried.

"But you must," said Evilina. "You've not yet had your First Bite. It'll keep you going."

They were interrupted by Dilly knocking on their door. She came in wearing her burger bar cap but with the peak at the back.

"Thought I'd drop in to tell you I got the kid back to her mum safely."

"So it was *you* in the burger bar last night!" said Evilina, looking at the cap.

"Yes," said Dilly. "You didn't know I'd been

following you disguised as a beggar-woman. Once I heard where you were going I flew ahead of the bus. And then I cast a spell to make Liz ill so I could get her job."

"But why?" asked Evilina.

"So I could do what Vlad told me to," said Dilly.

"What *are* you talking about?" said Evilina.

"Vlad told me to get a steak through Viktor's stomach. So, in the burger bar, I cast a spell to make him eat some…"

"EAT!" screamed Evilina, rushing at her and shaking her by the shoulders. "EAT! Are you mad? You didn't eat it, did you Viktor?"

"I…I…didn't eat the steak-burger."

"Thank Badness!" said Evilina, releasing her grip on Dilly. "So much for your spells, Dilly! What a narrow escape!" she said, sinking down into an armchair. "I feel quite dizzy. Dilly, run to your cousin and ask her for some snake oil to rub on my forehead."

Dilly, who still looked shaken, staggered to the door saying, "I think I need some too."

Though Viktor had answered Evilina's question it seemed to him, listening to her quarrelling with Dilly, as if he was watching a scene from a film. He didn't feel part it.

"Must be because I'm beginning to think like a human being," he said to himself. He understood why Evilina was so angry yet, at the same time, he was bored by all the fuss she was making.

Poor old Dilly, he thought, pity I can't tell her how grateful I am to her. I'm glad she cast that spell trying to make me eat the steak-burger and bumped into me when I had a piece of tomato on my fork. It gave me the idea of eating in order to become a human being. If it hadn't been for her I might not have thought about it.

Then he remembered her chanting in the middle of a grey mist just like the one that surrounded her when she was casting a spell to talk with his father.

"Wonder if there's any connection between those two spells?" he muttered. "Mum," he said, as the door closed behind Dilly, "I think she did see Dad the other night. You were trying to get the television to work but I was watching her and saw a dark figure near her. When you said 'Ask him what we should do?' the television was crackling and she probably didn't hear you clearly so she actually asked: 'What happened to you?' Can't understand why Dad answered that question by talking about a steak."

Evilina stared at him for some time. Then she covered her face with her hands and began to cry. Viktor found a box of cobwebs and handed her one but it took a long time before she'd recovered enough to speak. At last, gulping and sniffing, she said, "Viktor, there's something I should have told you…your father didn't come back to Vampsville because…because he…" her voice dropped to a whisper. "He got a stake through his heart!"

Suppose she thinks I'm going to be horrified, he thought. Maybe I would if I was still a vampire. Don't know what I can say to her.

He tried to look amazed but his voice was calm when he said, "It must have been dead tough for you, Mum. But it does explain things. Dad said 'stake' and Dilly thought he meant 'steak'. You always said she was useless at spelling and never listened carefully."

"You don't seem to be very upset!" said Evilina. "What's wrong with you? Don't you understand that it's a terrible disgrace and no-one must know?"

"Can't see why not," said Viktor.

"You must be much sicker than I thought," said Evilina, looking at him closely. "You're looking so human-like. If only you'd managed to get your First Bite! We'll just have to go back to the Morgans this evening."

"But you said…"

"Don't worry. I'll think up some excuse to explain why I left the hospital in a hurry…I'll say…"

I've got to tell her now that she's wasting her time, thought Viktor. And it's too late. I'm a human being and nothing can change that. He took a deep breath and began, "Mum. Got something to tell you.

In the burger bar…"

"Here it is!" said Dilly, rushing in with a large black jar.

"Ah, Dilly," said Evilina. "Never mind the snake oil. Tell me what you said to Jill last night."

"Just that I'd brought Maggie back because you had to take Viktor home."

"Well done, Dilly!" said Evilina, patting her on the back.

Dilly looked scared and moved away from her. Then she realised that Evilina was pleased with her and an enormous smile spread across her face and stayed there.

"Bob's nice," she said. "I sat on his bed and we played noughts and crosses. He won every time. He asked me to come again – I think he likes me."

"Hm, fellow-feeling probably," said Evilina. "He struck me as a remarkably stupid boy. But it gives me an idea. Dilly, how would you like to come with us to the Morgans this evening? Then you could go with Jill to visit Bob."

"Could I?" said Dilly.

"Of course," said Evilina. "Off you go and tidy yourself up."

Dilly went, with the smile still on her face, closing the door quietly behind her.

"Listen," said Evilina. "You, Dilly and I will go to the Morgans tonight. I'll say we've called to see if

Maggie's O.K. after I rescued her from the fire."

Viktor stared at her. "WHAT?"

"I'll tell Jill that I didn't go back to the ward because, when I looked out of the loo window, I saw smoke billowing from the burger bar and I rushed out to save you two. I asked Dilly to take Maggie back to her and I took you home immediately because you were suffering from post-traumatic stress."

"What's that?"

"Not sure really but they talk about it a lot in hospital dramas."

"Do you think Jill will believe you?"

"Why not? She should be very grateful and trust me all the more. Then I'll get Dilly to ask to see Bob. And once they've gone we can carry out the plan I had for last night."

No use trying to tell her anything, thought Viktor. I'm too tired and cold to argue and, besides, I'm longing to get back to the human world.

"What about Dilly? How will she get away from Jill?" he asked.

"Oh, as they leave the hospital she can tell her she's going late-night shopping."

When Dilly came back later the smile was still on her face.

"Ooh, Evilina!" she said. "Could we go by bus? I've never been on a bus."

Viktor was pleased that Evilina agreed because he knew he could no longer fly.

"It will be a good opportunity, Dilly, to explain my plan to you. You won't have to say anything except that you're only with us because you're so keen to see Bob again. Leave the rest of the talking to me.

"Now, Viktor, ready? This time it will have to be a case of third time lucky."

# CHAPTER 17

"Evie! Vic! What a lovely surprise!" said Maggie when she opened the front door. "And Dilly too! Bob kept talking about you after you left."

"Did he?" said Dilly. "Evilina has told me to...Ow!" she broke off as Evilina kicked her sharply on her ankle.

"Mum!" called Maggie. "Mum! It's Evie with Vic and Dilly!"

Jill came into the hallway and scowled at them. "Go away!" she said.

"Oh Mum! They won't hurt us. Please let them come in. It's so cold outside!"

"Oh, very well then," said Jill, taking them into the kitchen. She didn't ask them to sit down but stood looking at them, her mouth set in a hard, straight line.

"I've come to explain about yesterday evening," said Evilina.

"Don't bother," said Jill, "Maggie's told me everything Vic told her in the burger bar – about your being vampires."

"WHAT!" cried Evilina, glaring at Viktor. "Oh, take no notice of him," she said. "Kids are always making up stories to get attention…"

"He was telling the truth," said Jill. "I'd had my doubts about you two since you rushed off like that on Bonfire Night and I found Maggie sitting looking stunned on her bedroom floor. I felt I'd rather not leave Maggie with you again, Evie. That was why I took you to the hospital with me. I thought she'd be safe with Vic in the burger bar – I mean it's not the sort of place where you'd try to get your First Bite, is it?"

Evilina, Viktor and Maggie stared at her. And for a few moments no-one spoke.

At last Evilina said, "How do you know about First Bite, Jill?"

"Because," said Jill, "because I was a vampire once. When I was a vimp, learning about the human world, I used to wonder what it felt like to eat. Then, on my first visit to my 'blood' relations, I felt so at home in the human world I wanted to stay. I liked the Morgan family and didn't want to bite their son Ben. So when he offered me half his bar of chocolate I ate it and became human. I stayed with them and later married Ben's older brother Tom…Being human is not easy but I've never regretted my choice."

A huge wave of relief and happiness swept over Viktor as he listened to what she said. Great! he thought. So I'm not the only one. That's just how I felt and that's just what I did. Now when I tell Mum she'll understand.

But Jill hadn't finished. "My real name is Bloodjilly," she said.

"Bloodjilly!" echoed Evilina. "Bloodjilly! I married your brother, Vlad – that makes us sisters-in-law – so Maggie and Vic are cousins."

Maggie and Viktor gave each other a high-five and shouted, "Ye-e-ess!"

"But where is Vlad?" asked Jill.

Evilina looked at her and mouthed the letters S.T.T.H.

"My poor brother," sighed Jill. "He visited me once when Bob was a baby and Tom was out. He told me about his wife and baby vimp. And he was just showing me how long his fangs had grown so he could collect extra blood for his vimp's transfusions when Tom came home unexpectedly. He took one look at Vlad's fangs and had a heart attack on the spot. I told Vlad not to come again. I thought it would be better if the kids didn't know anything about the vampire world or what caused their father's death."

Once again Evilina, Viktor and Maggie were silent, thinking about what she'd said.

"So you really are my Aunt Evie," said Maggie.

"I wondered why you bit Vic's neck," Evilina said to her. "That explains it. There's still a touch of the vampire in you."

"Hm," said Jill. "There seems to be more than a touch of human being in Vic. He looks a lot different from how he did yesterday. His face is rounder and got more colour in it. Vic, what did happen at the burger bar last night?"

"He didn't eat anything," said Evilina. "He told me he didn't."

"I...I...I said I didn't eat the steak-burger when Dilly cast her spell."

Dilly looked up when she heard her name. For once she'd done exactly what she'd been told and had said nothing. While the rest of them had been talking she'd been busy blowing bubbles with the washing up liquid.

"But..." went on Viktor, "I did eat a piece of tomato."

"WHAT!" screamed Evilina. "But why? Why Viktor?" She shook her head. "No, no need to tell me...Jill's said it all...I suppose I should have known. The signs – no fangs and your blood allergy – were there right from the start. Always thought there was something strange about Vlad's side of the family."

Jill laughed. "We are an unusual family so maybe it's in Viktor's genes."

Viktor looked down at his frayed jeans but, before he could speak, Evilina said,

"That's all very well Jill, but where is he to live? I can't take him back with me. He'd be in terrible danger. The others would smell blood and attack him. You understood that and never tried to come back."

"He must stay here with us," said Jill. "We're his family, aren't we? And we'd love to have him."

Viktor could scarcely believe his ears. I always wanted to be friends with human beings, he thought, but this is loads better. I'll be part of a human family and live with them. He looked at Maggie. Her eyes were shining and there was a big grin on her face. But he noticed Evilina was unusually quiet.

"It does seem like a good solution," she said hesitantly. "At least I could make sure you never have to struggle again. Remember, living underground, we're always coming across buried treasure so you'll have everything money can buy. You could begin with a dishwasher," she said, looking at the plates piled up in the sink.

But there was something still puzzling Viktor.

"Mum," he said, "If Bob and I were little at the same time, how come I'm a hundred and he's only ten?"

"We measure time differently in our different worlds. You'll learn," said Evilina. She gave a deep sigh. "I shall miss you. And I shall miss you and Maggie too, Jill."

"It'd be great if you – and of course Dilly – could stay here, Evilina, but as Full-Blooded Vampires I

Rachel Adams

know you can't. But you will visit us, won't you? To see how Vic's growing up…and…we two got on well together – at least in the beginning…"

"Of course," said Evilina. "I'll pop in for a bit each evening."

"Do you mean you'll pop in for a *bite*," said Viktor, his brown eyes twinkling.

"As we're all related none of you is in any danger from me," said Evilina.

"And when Bob comes home, you must visit him, Dilly," said Jill, giving Evilina a look which showed she didn't think Bob would be in any danger from Dilly.

"Love to," said Dilly, "then we can play noughts and crosses again."

"Now, Dilly," said Evilina, "we really must be off. We'll walk to the end of the street. Don't want to frighten your neighbours, Jill."

At the front door Evilina hugged Jill and Maggie saying, "See you tomorrow night." Then she kissed Viktor and held him close to her for some time murmuring, "My little vimp!"

It was only as he stood on the doorstep and saw Evilina and Dilly walk away without him that he realised his life had changed forever.

I'll be seeing them again, he thought, but it won't be the same.

And by the time he watched them soaring over the rooftops tears were trickling down his cheeks.

Jill put an arm round his shoulders. "Cheer up, dear," she said. "One of the things you'll learn about being human is that you feel things more deeply but your feelings can change from one moment to the next. Don't worry. I'll be here to help you and so will Maggie."

"Mum," said Maggie. "Can I take Vic over to the allotment tomorrow? We could decide what to plant."

"Of course," said Jill, "but let's go in – it's so cold out here. Hot cocoa anyone?"

Viktor smiled at the mention of cocoa. No fear of sleeping pills in it and, this time, he'd really be able to drink it. Jill was right. His feelings had changed quickly. He began to think of all the exciting things he'd be able to enjoy now that he was human.

Although it was a cold November evening, he was already looking forward to eating blood-red raspberries with Maggie in the sunshine.

Printed in Great Britain
by Amazon.co.uk, Ltd.,
Marston Gate.